Louisa's Secret

For Miriam Hodgson

LITTLE SWAN BALLET BOOKS
1 Little Swan
2 Louisa's Secret
3 Louisa in the Wings
4 Louisa and Phoebe

A Red Fox Book

Published by Random House Children's Books
20 Vauxhall Bridge Road, London SW1V 2SA

A division of Random House UK Ltd
London Melbourne Sydney Auckland
Johannesburg and agencies throughout the world

Copyright © text Adèle Geras 1997
Copyright © illustrations Karen Popham 1997

5 7 9 10 8 6 4

First published in Great Britain by Red Fox 1997

Printed and bound in Great Britain by Cox & Wyman Ltd, Reading, Berks

Papers used by Random House UK Limited are natural, recyclable products made from
wood grown in sustainable forests. The manufacturing processes conform to the
environmental regulations of the country of origin.

RANDOM HOUSE UK Limited Reg. No. 954009

ISBN 0 09 921832 1

RANDOM HOUSE UK Limited Reg. No. 954009
ISBN 0 09 921822 4

RED FOX BALLET BOOKS

Louisa's Secret

by Adèle Geras

illustrated by Karen Popham

RED FOX

Chapter One

1 have to take good care of my legs and feet because when I grow up, I want to be a ballerina. I've been going to classes for three months now, and I've already danced in a show, so I'm a sort of ballerina already. Mrs Posnansky, our neighbour, says I am. She always calls me 'Little Swan', because that's what I was in the piece my class performed. Mrs Posnansky is from Russia, and her mother was in the corps de ballet, ages and ages ago, so she ought to know who is a real ballerina and who isn't. When I was being a Little Swan, she gave me the feathered headdress her mother used to wear, and she said I could keep it for ever and ever. I put it in a special box at the bottom of my cupboard, and it's my Very Favourite Thing.

If I didn't have to take care of my feet, I would have kicked my sister Annie under the table at supper. She called me Weezer. She *keeps* calling me Weezer, and I wish she wouldn't. I've explained to her over and over again that it's not the kind of name a ballet dancer would have. Louisa is my real name, and I don't see why she can't use it.

"Louisa Blair," I told her. "That's my name. It's a very good name for a dancer."

"I'm sorry," she said. "Only I've got used to Weezer. I've called you that for seven years, so it's hard to change all at once."

"You've got to try," I said. "You've got to get used to Louisa."

"OK," said Annie. "Louisa it is."

There was something very important I wanted to talk to her about. I said, "Were you here when they moved in next door?"

"No," said Annie. "I was at school, like you."

The house next to ours had been for sale for a long time, but it was sold a couple of months ago, and since then, I'd spent hours imagining the kind of family that would come and live there. I wanted them to have a child: someone I could play with, maybe even someone who could come to ballet class with me. I wanted them to have a pet, so that our cat, Brad, would have a friend as well. I used to discuss all this with Annie, usually while we were lying in bed, waiting to fall asleep. She said once, "Perhaps a handsome widower will move in, and Mum can marry him."

"Then he'd be a sort of dad," I said, "and we've got a dad, even if he and Mum are divorced. What do we want another one for?"

"Ours lives miles away," Annie said. "And I think Mum gets lonely sometimes."

"No, she doesn't," I said. "She's got us, hasn't she?" I didn't want to talk about Mum, so I said, "What will we do when the new people move in? Will we just go round there and knock at the door, and invite them to our house? I don't want to go on my own. We'll go together. OK?"

"OK."

"Promise?"

Annie sighed. She sighs quite a lot when I'm talking to her. "I promise. Go to sleep, Weezer."

"LOUISA!"

"Sorry . . . Louisa."

That was a few nights ago. Now I said, "Do you think we can go and say hello?"

Mum was in the kitchen, and she didn't wait for Annie to answer. "Certainly not," she said. "They'll be busy unpacking and getting everything straight. Tomorrow will be time enough for visits."

"But what if they've got lots of little kids all getting under their feet? They'd be glad to have them coming here for a bit, wouldn't they?"

"They haven't got lots of little kids," Mum said. "They've only got one, as far as I could see."

"A girl?" I held my breath and crossed my fingers behind my back for good luck.

"'Fraid not," said Mum. "A boy. With very dark hair."

I sniffed. I didn't care what colour his hair was, he was still a boy. "He won't want to play with me," I said. I'd have to stop daydreaming about a new friend.

"Why ever not?" Mum asked. "Boys like playing too, don't they?"

"Most of the time they like playing with other boys though, don't they? And I can't play football and climb trees, can I?"

"Why not?" Annie asked. "You used to like doing things like that. You're a fast runner, too."

"That was before I started ballet. I can't do those things now."

"Why not?"

Did she *really* have to have everything

explained to her? "Because," I said, "I mustn't injure myself. You can't dance if you're injured. And anyway, I haven't got time. I have to practise every day."

No one who isn't a dancer understands properly. They say they do, but they don't. You have to do exercises EVERY SINGLE DAY. The class is once a week, and lots of people who go to it do the barre exercises in class, but I do mine every single day, and sometimes I do them twice. In every book I've read about real ballet dancers, it says that you have do this if you are a 'truly dedicated dancer' and that's what I am. Even Tricia and Maisie, who are my very best friends, only really like going to class so that they can chat to everyone and dress up in satin shoes and pink leotards and things. When they come to my house, I make them join in dances I've made up, but I know they don't spend every spare minute thinking about being famous. They've both told me what they want to be when they grow up. Tricia wants to be a vet, and Maisie wants to be a nurse. I'm the only one who is determined to be a Prima Ballerina.

"Look!" Annie said suddenly, interrupting my thoughts. "Weezer, he's in the garden.

Come over here."

I was in such a rush to see our new neighbour that I forgot to tell Annie off for calling me Weezer. I stood next to her and stared out of the window.

The boy was small, about my size, and skinny, and he did have very dark hair.

"I wish he'd turn round," Annie said, "then we could see his face."

"I'm going out to talk to him," I said. "Are you coming?"

"No, you go by yourself. Go on. He might be a bit nervous if there's two of us."

"I don't see why he should."

"He shouldn't but he might. Go on, you go. Find out what his name is."

The boy didn't look like someone to be scared of, so I went. The hedge between our garden and his garden was quite low, so I could just see over the top.

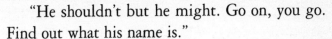

"Hello," I called out. "My name's Louisa Blair. What's your name?" I wasn't scowling.

Annie says I often scowl, so I made sure to smile my very best and friendliest smile.

The boy turned round. He had a nice face, for a boy, with blue eyes and pink cheeks. He looked a bit nervous, but he was grinning (sort of) and he said, "Tony. I mean that's my name."

"Tony what?"

"Tony Delaney."

"How old are you?"

"I'm eight. Are you eight?"

"Nearly," I said. "I'm very nearly eight. Have you got any brothers or sisters?"

"No. Have you?"

"Annie's my sister. She's ten. Have you got any pets?"

"No. Have you?"

"We've got a cat called Brad. It's short for Bradman. You'll see him soon. He likes your garden. What school do you go to?"

"I'm staying at St Cuthbert's for this term. That's the school I went to when we were in our old house. Then next term, I'm starting at Fairvale Junior."

"That's my school!" I said. "It's nice there. You'll like it."

"I won't know anyone," Tony said. He looked sad.

"You'll know me," I told him, but it didn't seem to cheer him up much. I added, "You can come and play in our house if you want."

"Really?" He looked happier at once. "I'll go and tell my mum."

He ran indoors and so did I. "He's coming," I said to Annie. "He's coming to play. I invited him. Is that OK, Mum?"

"Fine dear," Mum said. "Give him a drink and a biscuit when he gets here."

Chapter Two

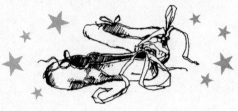

You *can* be friends with a boy. I didn't think you could, but you can. It all depends on the boy. Tony is a very good person to have as a friend, and because he lives so close to us, it means we can spend a lot of time together, either in his house or in mine.

"You really like him," Annie said to me one night, after he'd been living next door for a couple of weeks.

"So?" I said. "So what? What's wrong with that?"

"Weezer's got a boyfriend . . . Weezer's got a boyfriend . . ." she started to chant. I couldn't believe how stupid she was! *And* she'd called me Weezer! I threw my hairbrush at her, and it hit her on the shoulder.

"Oww!" she cried. "That hurt."

"Then stop being silly. Of course Tony isn't my boyfriend. He's a friend of mine, that's all.

And DON'T call me Weezer."

"All right," said Annie, jumping into her bed and pulling the duvet up to her shoulders. "Honestly! Can't you even take a joke?"

While I was falling asleep, I thought about Tony and why I liked him so much. There were three main reasons:

1. He always played any games I said we should play.

2. He didn't think boys were better than girls.

3. He never got cross, whatever you said to him.

"He's coming to play tomorrow," I said to Annie. "We're going to make a den at the bottom of the garden. It'll be our secret place."

"How can it be secret," Annie asked, "if you've already told me about it?"

"You must promise not to tell anyone. Do you promise?"

"OK," said Annie. "Now go to sleep."

We didn't make the secret den the next day. It was pouring with rain.

"We'll do it another day," Tony said.

"I wanted to do it today," I said. I really hate it when I can't do what I want to do when I want to do it, but Tony never seems to mind a bit. I felt quite annoyed with him. I said, "What are we going to do instead, then?"

"We can play board games," Tony said.

"I hate board games."

"Then I'll show you some card tricks."

"Don't want to learn card tricks."

"Come over to my house and we'll play some computer games."

Tony was better at computer games than I was, but I felt silly saying no over and over again, so I agreed.

Tony's house looked like our

house, but it was much tidier. Mrs Delaney is much fussier than my mum, but I like her. For instance, in Tony's house, we can't take drinks or biscuits or anything up to his room. We have to sit in the kitchen and eat properly at the table.

Tony loves his computer games, but I can never see the point of them. All these little figures just race about on the screen, and you have to zap them. I asked Tony, "Why do I have to zap them?"

"Because they're the baddies. And the more baddies you zap the more points you get."

I zapped for a while, but it soon got boring. "I know," I told Tony, "come back to my house and we'll watch videos."

"What videos have you got?" he asked.

"All sorts," I said. "Come on."

"OK." Tony switched the

17

computer off, and followed me to our house and into the lounge. There he was, agreeing with me again. Why didn't he care whether he got his own way or not? I decided to ask him. I said, "Tony, why don't you mind what games we play or what we do?"

He thought about this for a few seconds, then he said, "Well . . . I suppose it's because I like doing most things . . ." His voice faded away.

"Don't you ever get cross and lose your temper?"

"Sometimes I do."

"When was the last time?"

"Years and years ago."

"Years ago? That's amazing!"

"Why is it amazing? When did *you* last lose your temper?"

I laughed. "Yesterday. Or maybe even this morning. I can't remember. I get cross all the time."

"You've never been cross with me," Tony said.

"That's because you let me do everything I want to do. And what I want to do now is watch this video. It's very special. You sit there and don't say a word."

Tony sat on the sofa. He was looking excited, and I felt a bit bad about the trick I was going to play on him. I knew he thought he was going to see a film. I knew he was going to be disappointed, but I thought the best thing was just to start the video going and hope for the best.

"What's this?" he asked after he'd been watching for a few seconds.

"It's my new ballet video."

"Your *what?*"

"Ballet video. It's special. This is a film of Rudolf Nureyev and Margot Fonteyn. They're ever so famous. You'll love it, honestly. They're brilliant."

"I bet I'll hate it."

"Bet you won't. Just watch for a bit. Go on, and then I'll put a film on, I promise. Just watch for a minute."

Tony didn't answer, but he didn't look happy. He looked more fed-up than I'd ever seen him.

The first dance was Rudolf Nureyev doing a piece from a ballet called *Le Corsair*.

"He's supposed to be a fierce pirate," I told Tony. He grunted. I said, "Stop grunting and just watch."

The music was a loud, leaping, brave sort of tune, and Nureyev jumped and turned so fast that he almost seemed to fly through the air.

"Just a few more minutes," I said, and looked over to make sure Tony wasn't too bored. He was leaning forward and staring at the screen.

"What's the matter?" I asked.

"Nothing," he said. "Can you rewind a bit and play this dance again?"

He made me play it again four times.

"You really like it, don't you?" I said.

"It's OK." He grinned at me. "Be even better to do it though. And I bet I could, too."

"Bet you couldn't. Loads of people think they can do ballet, but it takes years and years of training. Fantastically *hard* training. It's ever so difficult."

"It can't be that difficult." Tony stood up. "I'm going to try."

"You can't try here," I said. "You'll bump into the furniture."

He looked out of the window. "We could go into the garden. It's not raining any more."

"But it's still wet. Your feet'll get stuck in the mud, and your trainers'll get dirty."

"Then let's go into the road."

We live on a little cul-de-sac off a main road, so I knew we weren't going to be run over, but I said, "Won't you be embarrassed? Leaping about for everyone to see? They'll think you're mad."

"No, they won't," Tony said. "It's nearly tea-time. Nobody'll be looking. Come on, I want to try it."

We went out of the front door very quietly. I didn't want Tony making a fool of himself. He made sure there were no cars anywhere, and then stepped into the road. After that, he started copying what he'd seen Rudolf Nureyev doing on the video. I couldn't believe my eyes. He wasn't anything like Nureyev, of course, but he *did* seem able to jump very high, and his legs were straight and the most amazing thing was, he knew where to put his arms, and I could see that he was staring at the same spot each time he turned round (which is the proper ballet way to stop yourself from getting dizzy).

"There," he said when he'd danced back to where I was standing. "What do you think of that?"

"You're a cheat. You've had lessons," I said. "You must have done."

"I haven't."

"Really?"

"Really."

"Then you should," I said. "Come with me tomorrow. Miss Matting always say she's short of boys."

"You won't catch me in a ballet class," he said. "That's for girly wimps."

I was so furious I nearly kicked him, but I remembered my feet just in time. I yelled at him instead. "It's *not* for girly wimps! It's for brilliant, strong, athletic people. And if it *is* for girly wimps, then you're the biggest girly wimp of all, because you won't even try. *You're* too scared to even come to class. And you've got a gift for it. You could be dead good."

"What would I tell my friends? They'd think I was soppy, going and dancing round with a lot of girls."

"*I* think you're soppy for caring what a lot

of stupid boys think."

"Well, I *do* care, so there. I'm sorry, Louisa. Dancing's fun, but I'd hate going to class, OK?"

I took a deep breath. Tony was beginning to sound quite cross. I wasn't going to get

anywhere with him if I went on and on about Miss Matting's. An idea had just come into my head. I put on my kindest, best voice. "OK," I said. "You don't have to come to class if you don't want to, but what if I taught you some stuff? I could teach you all the things we do. How about that?"

"What sort of things?"

"Everything. We'll start with the five positions for the feet. You've got to know what they are. Come on."

"Can't I do some more jumping?"

"Tomorrow," I said. "We've got to begin at the beginning. Miss Matting says a good foundation is very important. Let's go to my house, because I've got the right music."

"Yes, Miss," said Tony, and followed me inside.

Chapter Three

Tuesday is my best day of the week because I go to ballet straight after school. Tricia's mum picks me up in the car at four. I always get my suitcase ready on Monday night before I go to bed. Miss Matting says that real ballet dancers always make sure their ribbons are properly sewn on, and that their leotards and cardigans are clean. For the last couple of weeks, I'd enjoyed the lessons even more than I usually do, because as well as concentrating on my own dancing, I was also watching Miss Matting to see what real ballet teachers did, and trying very hard to remember all sorts of things which I could pass on to Tony at home.

He was a very good pupil. I never had to show him anything more than once. Miss Matting didn't tell us how good we were very often, but I told Tony all the time. I thought he'd like it. I also never stopped nagging him about coming to class with me, but nothing I said made any difference. I'd made him watch all kinds of videos, and he liked them a lot, and copied steps from them, but he wouldn't come to Miss Matting's with me, whatever I said to him.

Then one day in the car on the way to our ballet class, Tricia said, "Miss Matting's going to tell us something exciting today, do you remember? I can't wait to see what it's going to be. Maybe there'll be another show."

"No," I said. "She only does one a year. It won't be that."

"Here you are, girls," said Tricia's mum. "I'll pick you up at six."

We ran into the changing room. I love getting changed for class. I've never told anybody, not even Annie, what I pretend while I'm getting ready. I pretend I'm in Russia, at a proper ballet school, and that this class is for all the dancers in the corps de ballet of a real company. I pretend that Miss Matting isn't Miss Matting at all, but some very famous ballerina who's too old to go on stage and is passing on her knowledge to the next generation. I don't know many Russian names, so I think of my self as Louisa Posnansky. I'm sure Mrs Posnansky wouldn't mind if she knew, only of course she never will know, because I'll never tell anyone.

We always do exercises at the barre first. Miss Matting had a barre put up along one wall, but there's no mirror we can look into, so I usually imagine that as well. Some people don't concentrate on the barre exercises, but I always do, and today I was listening extra carefully to everything Miss Matting was saying, because I knew I'd have to go back and teach Tony all the things I'd learned.

"Back straight, Linda . . . Keep your toes pointed, really pointed, Alan . . . Jane, bend your knees, please, and lift, lift that arm . . . Grace and poise, Pamela, you're not about to throw a javelin, dear!"

After the barre exercises, we did more exercises in the middle of the room. I pretended I had blocked shoes on, and was going to do point work, even though I knew it would be years and years before I was really allowed to go up on my toes. It's only when your feet have grown strong that you can dance like that, and lots of girls don't understand this and try to go up on points much too early.

After the exercises were finished, we all sat on the floor. Miss Matting said, "Well, I

promised you a surprise last week, and now I'm ready to tell you about it. I think you're all ready to make up a little dance of your own. I want you to do it in pairs, please, and I'll ask to see your efforts in three weeks. So, find a partner and being to think about it. Please choose someone who can practise with you at home because, of course, there won't be time during class and in any case, I wish to be amazed by your performances. Making up the steps of a dance is called 'choreography', as I'm sure many of you know, so I want you all to become choreographers as well as dancers. Keep it simple and about three minutes long, please. It sounds like a very short time, but I promise you, once you start to plan your steps it'll turn out to be much longer than you think."

The moment Miss Matting started to tell us her surprise, I knew exactly what I was going to do. I'd make up a dance for me and Tony. In my head, I could see myself wearing a pale lilac tutu with roses in my hair, and Tony dressed in a blue velvet jacket. We weren't going to be dancing in costume, of course, but I couldn't help imagining it. I was going to dance with him and no one else.

"Will you be my partner?" Tricia asked.

"No, Weezer, be mine," Maisie begged.

"Louisa," I said, but I was so busy day-dreaming that I knew I didn't sound even a bit cross. "No, I'm sorry, Tricia, I'm really sorry, Maisie, but you two will have to do your dance together. I've got a secret partner."

"Who is it?" Maisie asked. "Is it Pam? Or Linda?"

"I'm not saying," I told her. "It wouldn't be a secret if I told you, would it?"

"I think you're a real meany," said Maisie, "not to tell us."

"It'll be a surprise," I grinned at her. "You'll see."

"Have you told anyone else?" Tricia asked.

"No," I said. "I might tell Annie. Or I might not. I'll decide later."

I did tell Annie. I told her all about it.

"But you must absolutely swear," I said, "not to tell a soul. Not a single, solitary soul."

Annie said, "OK, but I don't see how you can possibly get away without telling Tony what he's doing."

"If he knew he was going to have to dance at my ballet class, he'd never agree. So I'm just going to pretend a bit, that's all."

"He's sure to find out," said Annie.

"No, he won't," I smiled at her. "Not if you don't tell him. I'll think of a story for him, don't worry."

"And what about Tricia and Maisie? They're always coming round here to play, and they're bound to find out that you and Tony are dancing together."

"I've thought of that," I said. "I'll go and play at their houses for a bit, that's all. I won't

tell them any lies. I'll tell them they can't come round here because I'm preparing something special for Miss Matting, but that it's a deadly secret, and that's true."

"Won't they be hurt?" Annie asked.

"Why should they be?" My sister has some very funny ideas sometimes.

"Because they're your friends and friends aren't supposed to keep things secret from one another."

"It won't be secret for ever," I told her.

"Anyway, they know it's a dance I'm hiding from them, and not anything else."

"You're hiding Tony from them too," Annie said.

I sighed. "I'll tell them everything in the end," I said. "Don't worry about it."

Tony was getting better and better.

"I'm really pleased with you," I told him. "You're getting to be a proper dancer. I'm going to take you to meet Mrs Posnansky."

"Oh no, Weezer, please . . . I don't know her . . . I've only ever said hello to her once. Why do I have to go?"

"LOUISA!" I shouted. Then I said, "If you don't call me Louisa, I'll call you Ant." I knew Tony hated being called Ant because he'd told me so. I went on, "The reason we have to go is because I want her to see what a good dancer you are. I've told her all about you and all about our lessons. Also, I want to ask her advice about something . . . steps and stuff."

"What does she know about ballet?"

"She knows a lot. Her mum was a proper dancer in a real ballet company."

"I know," Tony said. "You showed me the headdress she wore in *Swan Lake* which Mrs Posnansky gave you . . . but I won't know what to say."

"I'll talk," I told him. "You won't have to say a thing."

Tony sighed. "Do I have to come?"

"Yes," I said. "You do. She always gives me chocolate. Sometimes she gives us cakes. And her house isn't like our house. It's different. You'll like it, you'll see. She won't eat you. She likes children."

"OK," said Tony. "I suppose I'll have to come or you'll never stop nagging me."

"That's right," I said. "I won't."

I knew the chocolate and cakes would persuade him. I think boys are greedier than girls.

Chapter Four

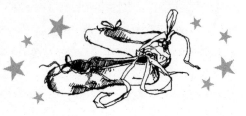

I love going to Mrs Posnansky's. Her house is more like a house in a fairytale than any other place I've ever seen. All her furniture is made of dark wood, and there are velvet curtains at the windows. She has lots of framed photographs up on the walls of her lounge, and Annie and I love looking at them. Everyone in them is dressed in old-fashioned clothes and some of the men have very long moustaches and they're wearing big fur hats because it's very cold in Russia during the winter.

Mrs Posnansky took one look at Tony sitting rather uncomfortably on the sofa and said to him, "Today I have special cinnamon cake. This you like?"

"Oh, yes please," he said. "That sounds lovely."

"My Little Swan . . . she likes my cakes."

Tony looked a bit puzzled, so I explained.

"Mrs Posnansky means me. She always calls me that. I was in the Dance of the Little Swans, you see."

"It suits her," Mrs Posnansky said. "She is full of gracefulness and has long white neck, like a swan. Also, like swan, she loves to eat. When she comes, I have chocolate. You like too?"

"Oh, yes," said Tony. "I like chocolate. I like it a lot."

"You shall have," said Mrs Posnansky. "After the cake. I will go and bring."

"I'll help you," I told her, then I turned to Tony. "Just wait here," I said to him. "I'll be back in a minute."

While I was alone in the kitchen with Mrs Posnansky, I told her all about my plan to make up a dance with Tony as my partner.

"But he won't come to the ballet class with me," I told her, "so what can I say to him? How can I make sure he agrees to dance with me?"

Mrs Posnansky was pottering around, opening and shutting drawers, filling the kettle, and putting a plate full of slices of cake on to a trolley, together with some glasses for

the lemon
tea she always
gives her visitors.

"Tell him," she
said, "that there is a
show somewhere. How do you say it? A competition to see who is best."

"You mean a talent contest?"

"I mean this . . . yes, my dear Little Swan. A talent contest."

"What a clever person you are!" I said. "Thank you."

"Not very clever," she said. "Only old. Now you help to push this trolley in for me, please."

Tony became a lot chattier after he'd eaten the cake, and by the time the chocolate came out, he and Mrs Posnansky were the best of friends.

"I hear from my dear Little Swan," she said,

"that you are very strong dancer."

"Oh, well," Tony said blushing. "Weezer exaggerates a bit sometimes."

"Louisa," I hissed.

"Sorry, Louisa . . . Yes, I like dancing. And she's a good teacher."

"This I am sure of," Mrs Posnansky said, smiling. "I am sure she is of the strictest kind with no nonsense. This is for ballet the best sort of teacher. A soft teacher is not so good."

"She's not soft," Tony said. "She makes me practise every day."

"So," said Mrs Posnansky, "I wait eagerly to see you dancing together. You will be good partners, yes?"

"I don't know really," said Tony. "I haven't ever danced with her . . . not properly."

"Well," I said, taking a deep breath to get me ready for the

lie I was going to tell, "when we go home, we're going to start working out a dance to do together. There's a talent contest in a couple of weeks and I'd love to win it. Wouldn't you?"

"A talent contest?" Tony's eyes shone. "With prizes?"

I hadn't thought about that. I didn't want to promise prizes that we were never going to get so I just said, "I don't know what the prizes are," and then I began to talk about something else. After a while, I said, "We must go home now, Mrs Posnansky."

"Yes," said Tony. "I want to go and start working on our dance."

Mrs Posnansky walked slowly to the door with us, leaning on her stick. "Goodbye, Little Swan, and goodbye, Tony," she said. "Please come to show me your dance when it is ready."

"We will," I told her. "Thank you for having us."

"Yes, thank you," said Tony, and Mrs Posnansky said, "It is always a pleasure," and she waved at us as we crossed the road.

"Have you thought about what we're going to do?" Tony said as soon as we were in the lounge of my house.

"Not really," I said. "The dance has got to be about three minutes long. That sounds like a tiny amount of time, but it's long when you have to fill it up with steps."

"Well, I've been thinking," Tony said.

"When have you been thinking?"

"Ever since you told me about it across the road . . . anyway, listen. I reckon it'd be a good idea if we . . . well, it sounds stupid, but what if we danced a whole story?"

"In three minutes?" I laughed. "You're barmy, honestly."

"No hang on. You don't understand. I mean a really short story."

"How short?"

"What about a nursery rhyme?"

"A nursery rhyme? Are you mad? Nursery rhymes are for babies!"

"But everyone knows them, and if we do the one I'm thinking of, it will give us a chance to do some really brilliant things . . . really difficult steps, I mean. And there won't be that many people doing ballet in the talent contest, so at least we'll be different."

I gasped. I'd almost forgotten about the talent contest. I said quickly, "Which nursery rhyme were you thinking of? I don't fancy being Miss Muffet."

"What do you think of Jack and Jill? We could have fun working it out."

"Let's try it," I said. "Jack and Jill . . . right. Well. Come on, give me your hand and we'll start by walking up the hill."

We worked out the steps for going up the hill and Tony thought of a clever extra bit where we both started pulling on the handle of a pretend bucket. Then we worked out how we'd look down an imaginary well, and how we'd take turns winding the handle to bring up our bucket of water.

"The hardest bit," said Tony, "will be tumbling down the hill. We don't want to hurt ourselves by falling properly."

"I know," I said. "Can you do cartwheels?"

"Yes," said Tony, "but that's not real ballet, is it?"

I didn't know if it was or not, but I knew that cartwheels were fun to do and I was good at them, so I said, "It's modern ballet. We can have a sort of quarrel over who's going to be carrying the bucket down the hill and then I'll give you a push and you can go into two or three cartwheels. Let's try it."

"I can only do one cartwheel in here." Tony said.

"Never mind. Let's just see what it looks like."

Tony grabbed hold of an invisible bucket that was very heavy. We took turns to pull at it, and then I gave him a tap on the shoulder. He raised his arms above his head, and then spun into a perfect cartwheel, ending up on the carpet with his arms and legs bent into a funny shape and his face twisted in pretend pain. I clapped my hands.

"That's lovely," I said. "I'm going to do that, too. Watch!"

I did a cartwheel and tried to copy Tony as closely as I could. I ended up next to him, clutching my back.

"Yes," he said. "It's going to be great." He stood up. "Now . . . we must work on those steps at the beginning."

Chapter Five

Tony and I practised every day. We found a piece of music that fitted the Jack and Jill story really well. It was a march by Chopin, and whenever I heard it, it made me feel like striding out, up the hill. We rehearsed our cartwheels in the garden.

"Are you sure," Tony asked, "that the stage will be big enough for us to do three cartwheels?"

"Don't worry," I said, and started talking about something else. I couldn't tell him we wouldn't be on a stage, but would have the whole length of St Christopher's church hall to do our dance in.

On the Monday afternoon before the class, we went over to show Mrs Posnansky what we'd been rehearsing. She clapped her hands and said we were magnificent and splendid, and she gave us some chocolate to take home.

When we were back at my house, we ate all the chocolate, and then Tony said to me, "What are you going to do about your ballet class tomorrow? You're going to have to miss it, aren't you? To do this talent contest. Won't Miss Matting be cross?"

"Umm . . . " I hadn't thought about this. I said, "Oh, I've already told Miss Matting. She doesn't mind at all. Not just for this once. And I've told Tricia not to pick me up in the car tomorrow."

This was true. I'd said that Annie was bringing me because she wanted to see the dances that everyone had made up.

"What do you think we should wear?" Tony asked. "For Jack and Jill. We haven't thought of that."

I knew I was supposed to wear my tights and leotard to class, but I *did* want us to look as much like a brother and sister as possible, and I knew we both had red tracksuits. I could have my ballet stuff on underneath, and take the tracksuit off when the dances were finished and the proper class began. But what if the dances came last, after we'd done all the exercises? And what if Tony took one look at St Christopher's and saw that I'd tricked him? I'd told him the talent contest was being held in the sports centre. He'd go straight home. He'd probably never speak to me again. I was beginning to think that having Tony as my partner was not such a bright idea, but then I remembered what a good dancer he was, and I decided that I'd *make* him come into the hall with me, whatever he said.

On Tuesday afternoon, it didn't take Tony very long to work out that we weren't walking towards the sports centre.

"This isn't the way to the sports centre," he said. "Where are you going?"

"It's a short cut," I told him, hurrying along the pavement so that I wouldn't have to talk to him.

"No, it's not," he said, a bit breathlessly. "The centre's over there. I've lived here long enough to know that much."

I didn't bother to lie any more. I just muttered, "We're nearly there now," and Tony said, "Nearly where? Honestly, Weezer, you are a pain sometimes! Where are we going?"

"It's a surprise," I said, "and don't call me Weezer!"

"OK," he said. "But tell me the truth. This

talent contest isn't being held at the sports centre at all, is it? You didn't want to tell me because you thought I'd only come if it *was* at the sports centre. Right?"

"Right. Look, come on," I said. "It's getting late. We'll be there in a minute."

I was busy wishing St Christopher's wasn't such a big and churchy-looking church. There it was, right bang slap in the middle of town and everyone knew it.

As soon as Tony saw it, he cried, "But that's St Christopher's! That's where you go to ballet!"

I nodded. He went on, "You go to ballet on Tuesdays at four."

I nodded again. I felt like closing my eyes because I didn't like the way Tony's face had gone quite white. He was starting to look really angry.

"I know what you've done. You've brought me to your ballet class. That's horrible of you, Weezer, and I'm going to call you Weezer because you don't deserve to be a Louisa. I thought you were my friend, but you tricked me! Well, I'm not going to jump around in front of a whole lot of stupid girls. I'm going home."

He turned round and started walking down the road. I went racing after him. He couldn't go now, not after all our work. I shouted, "Tony! Stop, Tony! Stop and listen to me . . . Just listen for a second . . . please."

He stopped, and looked at me. He was still angry, but at least he seemed ready to listen.

"Tony, I'm sorry. I didn't like lying to you, but I had to do it, didn't I? When Miss Matting said we had to find someone to dance with, I just knew it had to be you because you're the best dancer I know. You're better than anyone else in my class . . . and I just thought we could do a really good dance."

I felt so sad when I thought that all our hard work had been for nothing that I started to cry. Tony came up to me and peered at my face.

"Don't cry. Please stop crying, Weezer. It's your own fault I won't come to your class. I said all along I wouldn't. Why are you crying?"

"I'm crying," I said, "because I've worked so hard and it's such a waste. You're a good dancer and you won't do anything about it. You worked hard too. *And* you enjoyed it, so don't say you didn't."

Tony sighed. He said, "All right, all right, I'll do it. I'll come into your class, just this once. Just stop crying, Weezer, please."

"OK," I said. "Thanks, Tony." I took my hankie out and blew my nose. I decided to ignore the Weezer. Tony was coming into my ballet class! I said, "It'll be fine, you'll see.

There *are* some boys in the class. I told you about them."

"Girly wimps!" he said, but he was smiling.

"No, they're not," I smiled back at him. "You'll see. They're ordinary boys like you. I'll take you in and introduce you to Miss Matting. I expect you'll have to wait to do our dance till we've done all our exercises."

Tony followed me into the hall. I'd made sure we were early, because I knew that I'd probably have to explain everything to Miss Matting.

"Hello, Louisa dear," she said, coming towards us as soon as she saw us come in. "Who is this young man?"

"It's Tony Delaney, Miss Matting."

"Hello, Tony," said Miss Matting.

"Hello," said Tony.

Nobody seemed to know what to do next, so I said, "Tony lives next door to me and we've made up a dance together."

"How delightful!" said Miss Matting. "I look forward to seeing it very much. You can sit on one of those chairs, Tony dear, just while we do our exercises."

Tony nodded and sat down. I ran to the

changing room to take off my red tracksuit. I'd have to put it on again for the Jack and Jill routine, but I didn't care. Tony was here. He was going to watch our class. He hadn't run away.

Tricia and Maisie were waiting for me in the changing room.

"It's Tony!" Tricia said. "He's your secret partner. Why didn't you tell us? We'd never have told anyone, honest!"

"Yes, but if I'd told you, then it wouldn't really have been a secret would it?" I said.

"I suppose not," said Maisie. "Is he a good dancer?"

"Wait and see," I said, and went into the hall to take my place at the barre.

Chapter Six

Tony and I had to wait until the very end of the class to do our dance. As soon as the exercises were over, Miss Matting said, "We'll have five minutes' rest everyone, and then I'll see your dances. I'm greatly looking forward to this, and I hope you are too."

I *was* looking forward to showing off our Jack and Jill dance, but while I was in the changing room getting into my tracksuit, I could feel my heart beating very hard in my chest. I went to sit next to Tony when I was ready, and I whispered to him, "I'm nervous. Are you?"

"No," said Tony. "Not really."

"Why not? Why aren't you?"

I couldn't understand Tony at all. He wasn't a bit like me. He never lost his temper – well, hardly ever – and now he was sitting here as calm as calm, not a bit worried about dancing in front of all these strangers.

I decided boys' minds just didn't work in the same way girls' minds did. I said, "Aren't you scared of forgetting the steps? Or falling over in the middle of a cartwheel?"

"Well," he said, "I know what we have to do. We've practised it enough, haven't we? We'll just do it the way we do it at home. I'm waiting to see what everyone else does. And guess what?"

"What?"

"I know James Williams."

"Really?"

"Yes, he goes to my school. He's in the class below me. I never knew he did ballet."

"He's not a silly boy," I said, "who thinks that only girly wimps do ballet."

"Ssh," said Tony. "They're starting."

Maisie and Tricia were the first pair to dance. They were pretending to be kittens. Linda and Pam were birds; two of the boys did a sailors' hornpipe. I watched each pair carefully, and they were all very good. I began to feel more and more nervous.

"No one's done a story yet," Tony whispered to me. "I think our dance is the best."

I thought that, too, only I'd never have said so to anyone except Annie. That doesn't really count, though, because she's my sister and I tell her everything.

Soon all the others had done their dances, and it was our turn.

"Louisa has brought a new boy to the class to be her partner, children," said Miss Matting. "Say hello to Tony Delaney, everyone."

Everyone said, "Hello Tony!" I thought he would be embarrassed, but he looked exactly the same as he always did, and he said "Hello," back to them.

I gave Miss Matting our music tape and she put it on for us. As soon as I heard the first chords, I forgot all about the others, and the room we were in, and Miss Matting. I even forgot about being the very best. I could almost see the steep hill in front of us, with the well at the top. When it came to pushing Jack, I held my breath for a moment, hoping that Tony wouldn't be put off his cartwheels by having to do them in a place he'd never even seen before, and on a surface he wasn't used to. I needn't have worried. He whirled along so fast that it really *did* look as though he were tumbling out of control, and when he landed at the bottom of the hill, the face he pulled as he clutched his sore head made the whole class laugh. They laughed again when I did my tumbling after, and when we'd finished, every-one clapped.

"Well," said Miss Matting, "I must say I'm very pleased with you all, class. You've worked very hard, and your dances were excellent, and I think Louisa and Tony were very clever to think of doing a whole story as a dance."

"It was Tony's idea," I said. "And he helped me with the choreography."

"It was a very good idea. Have you been going to ballet classes for long, Tony?"

"No, Miss Matting," he said.

"He's never been," I said. "I taught him all the positions and steps. I try to remember everything that you show us in class, and then I go home and teach it to Tony. He lives next door to me, so we can practise every day."

"Well, you're a very good teacher, Louisa. Maybe I'll take a holiday and leave you in charge."

"Oh no," I said. "I want to learn, Miss Matting. I don't want to teach."

"I was only joking, dear. Of course I shall go on teaching you all. But Tony, I would be very pleased if you joined the class. I think you've got a real gift and it would be a shame if you didn't develop it, don't you think?"

"Yes, Miss Matting, I suppose so," Tony said.

"So will you come every week? There's always a shortage of good male dancers, you know."

Tony looked at me and hesitated. I nodded at him. He turned back to Miss Matting and grinned at her. "OK. I mean, yes, I'd really like to come and learn properly. I'll ask my mum and dad tonight."

I was so happy that Tony was going to come to class with me every Tuesday that it wasn't

until we were back at home and telling Annie
all about it that I realised
what he'd said to Miss
Matting.

"You told Miss
Matting you wanted to
learn properly. Does that
mean you think I don't
teach you properly?"

"No, no, of course not," he said. "You've taught me brilliantly. Really you have. And I'm glad I'm coming to class with you on Tuesdays."

"Me and all the girly wimps," I said. "Don't forget them."

"I'm going home now," he said, "to ask my mum and dad, and tell them all about our dance."

He did some Nureyev-style leaps as he made his way to the front door and frightened poor Brad who was lying on the mat at the bottom of the stairs.

"Sorry, Brad," said Tony. "I didn't mean to scare you. 'Bye, Weezer."

"'Bye, Ant." I stuck my tongue out at him. "See you tomorrow."

That night in bed I said to Annie, "Miss Matting thinks Tony has a real gift. She said so."

"Well, you said so as well. Didn't you?"

"But I'm worried now," I said.

Annie groaned. "Honestly, you find things to worry about that no one else has ever thought of before. What is it now?"

"What if he's better than I am?" I said. "I don't mind him being gifted, but I want to be even more gifted."

"He's a boy," Annie said. "It's different. No one will be comparing him with you. And Margot Fonteyn had Rudolf Nureyev, didn't she? A real, proper ballerina needs a good partner. You told me that. You're always telling me that."

I closed my eyes and thought about this for a bit. I could see Tony and me taking a bow on a big stage with red velvet curtains behind us, just like Fonteyn and Nureyev.

"Blair and Delaney," I told Annie. "It has to be that way round – Louisa Blair and Tony Delaney – doesn't it?"

"Of course it does," said Annie. "It wouldn't be at all the same if his name came first. Now go to sleep, Weezer, it's late."

I was falling asleep as Annie was talking. I don't even know if she heard me saying, "Louisa . . . my name's Louisa," or if I was only thinking it in my head.

Red Fox Ballet Books

The perfect read for budding ballerinas!

Little Swan by Adèle Geras

Louisa has just started ballet lessons and she's determined to be top of the class. So when performance time comes, she knows there is only one role for her – prima ballerina (or else!).

£2.99   ISBN 0 09 921822 4

Louisa's Secret by Adèle Geras

Louisa's new neighbour is great. There's only one problem – he's a boy, and boys and ballet don't mix, or do they?

£2.99   ISBN 0 09 921832 1

Louisa in the Wings by Adèle Geras

When a famous Russian ballet company comes to town, Louisa just has to see them. Can she get the money for the tickets in time? Or is the show destined to go on without her?

£2.99   ISBN 0 09 921842 9

A Rival for Louisa by Adèle Geras

Phoebe's new to the ballet class and Louisa takes an instant dislike to her – she's pretty, posh and, worst of all, a good dancer, too! Can they learn to put their differences aside and become friends?

£2.99   ISBN 0 09 921852 6